The Belgium Book Mystery

The Belgium Book Mystery

Stacy Towle Morgan

Illustrated by Pamela Querin

BETHANY HOUSE PUBLISHERS
MINNEAPOLIS, MINNESOTA 55438

Published by Bethany House Publishers
A Ministry of Bethany Fellowship, Inc.
11300 Hampshire Avenue South
Minneapolis, Minnesota 55438

Printed in the United States of America.

Library of Congress Cataloging-in-Publication Data

Morgan, Stacy Towle.
    The Belgium book mystery / Stacy Towle Morgan.
        p.   cm. — (The Ruby Slippers School ; 2)
    Summary: Eight-year-old Hope Brown and her younger sister
Annie go to Belgium with their parents in hopes of finding out who
has been sabotaging the printing operation of friends who run a
Christian press.

    [1. Series—Fiction. 2. Christian life—Fiction. 3. Belgium—
Fiction. 4. Mystery and detective stories.] I. Title. II. Series:
Morgan, Stacy Towle. Ruby Slippers School ; 2.
PZ7.M82642Be   1996
[Fic]—dc20   95–43933
ISBN 1–55661–601–5   CIP
                                                                  AC

To Dad and Mom—

for sharing with me

many late-night strolls

through the Grand' Place.

STACY TOWLE MORGAN has been writing ever since she was eight, when she set up a typewriter in the closet of the room she shared with her sister. A graduate of Cedarville College and Western Kentucky University, Stacy has written many feature articles and several books for children. Stacy and her husband, Michael, make their home in Indiana, where she currently spends her days home-schooling their four school-aged children in their own Ruby Slippers School.

Ruby Slippers School

Adventure in the Caribbean

The Belgium Book Mystery

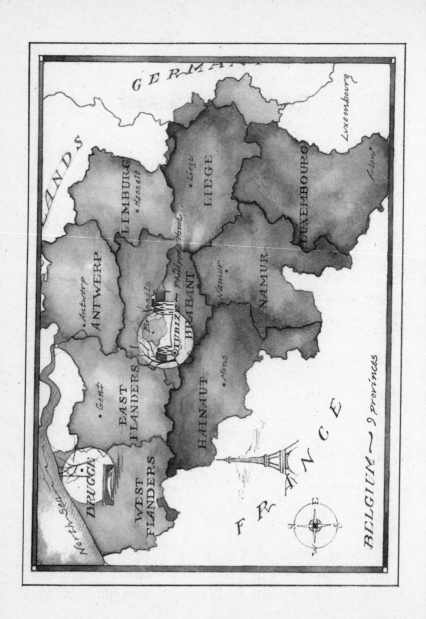

Prologue

My name is Hope Vivian Brown, and I'm eight and one-quarter years old. My little sister, Annie, is nearly seven—you can see why the one-quarter is so important! I was only fifteen months old when she was born and was too little to remember much. My mom told me what it was like the day my dad and I went to bring Mom and Annie home from the hospital.

That was the day I got Ellsworth, my bear. That also was the day I got my finger caught in the car door and went to the emergency room and got stitches. I remember Dad holding a towel over my finger and promising that the four of us would go out for ice cream after it was all over. My mom said I only cried for a minute during the stitches, but Annie screamed the whole time afterward at the ice-cream parlor.

Some things never change. If I move up to the blue lesson book in piano, Annie wants to move up, too. If I get to talk to Nana on the phone, Annie wants to talk a little longer than I did. Because we're home-schooled, we do almost everything together—including argue. But when we're not arguing, we're the best of friends. And when we travel together with Mom and Dad, we're especially good friends because there usually isn't anyone else to talk to!

My dad has a job where he travels a lot. He's a time-management consultant. That's just a fancy word that means he helps companies all over the world get the most work done in the shortest time. He has a sign on his office wall that reads "Time is money." If that's the case, Annie and I are really rich, because we get to spend lots of time with Mom and Dad. I think that's the best part about home-schooling. We're always learning something new. Just wait until you hear about our latest adventure!

Chapter One

It was Christmas Eve. Annie and I were admiring our new Christmas ornaments on the tree. Every year, all four of us in our family go shopping to pick out an ornament for ourselves. When we get home, Mom takes out a permanent marker and writes our name and the year on the bottom of the ornament. This year, she reminded us that we can take them with us when we grow up and leave home.

"After all, by then you each should have at least twenty ornaments—enough to decorate your first tree."

Dad picked up my angel from three years ago and cradled her in his hand. "Someday, this angel will hang on your own little tree in your own home. At least your Christmas tree will have company even if you don't," he joked.

"You mean you're not going to come visit me at Christmastime when I'm grown-up?" I asked.

Dad grabbed me around the waist and hugged me. "Well, I guess we'll have to, just to see that tree of yours!"

"Your new ornament sure does sparkle, Hope," Mom added. "I love the one you picked out this year. It's got the perfect spot."

I stood back and looked at my silver snowflake, glimmering against the white lights. Out of the corner of my eye, I could see Annie sitting in the corner chair. Frowning, her arms were crossed tightly against her chest.

"That's because Hope hogged the best place," she said. "I would have put my jack-in-the-box there, but she ran in ahead of me and took the branch I wanted."

"That's not true!"

"Is so."

"Is not."

"Is so."

"Hey, wait a minute! Listen to yourselves. You sound like two-year-olds," Dad said as he stepped between us. "I can't believe you're fighting about a branch on the tree. There are plenty of spots to hang your ornaments. What's wrong with this one here?" He pointed to an empty space down and to the left of where my snowflake dangled.

"That's no good, Dad," Annie whined. "The

14

branch bends as soon as I put my jack-in-the-box on it. My ornament is too heavy."

"OK, so why don't you and Hope switch? Her snowflake is light and can go here, and your jack-in-the-box is heavy, so it can go there. All settled."

That's when I ran out of the room.

I can just imagine the conversation after I left. It probably went something like this: Mom must have said, "I saw that coming." Dad would ask, "What's wrong with Hope?" and Annie would smugly say, "I think that looks *much* better."

Sometimes being the big sister can be really tough. It seems as if I always have to give in and let Annie have her way. It's not easy living with an almost seven-year-old!

I picked up Ellsworth, my bear, and held him close. "Be glad you don't have a little sister," I whispered. "They can be a real pain in the neck."

Just then, the doorbell rang, and I could hear the sound of Christmas carols coming from outside. As I ran to my bedroom window to look out, Mom called up the stairs, "Hope, come on down and see who's here!"

I opened the window and felt a blast of cold air. The sounds of "Joy to the World" floated up to my window. I sure didn't feel joyful tonight.

At that moment, Annie opened my bedroom door and poked her head in. "C'mon, Hope. They'll leave before you get down to hear them."

"I'm coming," I said reluctantly.

As I followed Annie down the stairs, the carolers started singing "Silent Night."

"Silent night! Holy night!
All is calm, all is bright
Round yon virgin mother and Child,
Holy Infant, so tender and mild—
Sleep in heavenly peace,
Sleep in heavenly peace."

I looked up past the carolers and saw the full moon and the bright stars. I started thinking about the Christmas story and the baby Jesus lying in the manger. *Of all the nights to be fighting with my sister,* I thought sadly.

Annie leaned against me and reached for my hand. "I'm sorry about what happened. I'll move my ornament if you want."

"That's OK, Annie. That's not what is really important," I said. And I realized it really wasn't.

Chapter Two

The next morning, Annie and I had already raced through our stockings before Mom and Dad finished getting film into the camera.

"Hold up your stocking, Annie," Mom said. "I want to get a picture of you with it."

"But it's already empty," Annie protested.

"That's OK. Aunt Lottie will enjoy seeing the stocking she made you when you were a baby. Stand next to Hope and smile."

Dad stood up and stretched. "I'm going to the kitchen to make coffee. Don't start tearing into those presents until I get back!"

There are two things I don't like about Christmas: It feels like it will never come, and then when it does, it's over too soon.

I picked up one of the boxes and shook it hard.

It was wrapped in green paper with the word *Noël* written all over it in gold. Annie had one just like it.

"You heard Daddy, don't start opening the presents yet," Mom warned. "Anyway, I want you to save that present until last."

I wondered what was taking him so long. I could already smell the coffee going in the kitchen. As I walked around the corner of the dining room, I heard Dad's voice. "I think everything is set. I guess we'll see you on the twenty-seventh. You sure you want to meet us at six in the morning? OK. Take care, Bill. Goodbye."

Dad hung up and turned around, looking a bit surprised. "Hey, what are you doing in here? How come you're not in there drooling—or should I say *dueling*—over the presents?"

"Annie and I aren't thaaaat bad." I was a little embarrassed about yesterday's fight and wanted to change the subject. "Who was that, Dad? Are we going somewhere?"

"I'll tell you later," he said, patting me on the head. He poured coffee into two mugs and started toward the other room. "C'mon, Hope, you're going to miss all the excitement. Let's go open some presents!"

Even though I had a great time opening gifts, I kept my eye on the green one Mom said I had to save until last. For once, I wasn't disappointed when the gift-giving was almost over and Dad handed me the

final present. "Here, girls. These are the last two gifts. One for each of you."

I felt a twinge of jealousy that we both were getting exactly the same present. I thought it would have been more special if mine had been the only one.

"Go ahead, Annie. You go first," I said, trying to save my present till last.

"No, you can go ahead. I'll wait."

"But I want you to go ahead!"

"But I don't want to," Annie said stubbornly.

I was determined to win this one. "I'm not going to open mine until you've opened yours," I said, hoping that would end it.

Mom was standing there with the video camera running. "I've got all this on tape. Would you like me to rewind it so you can see yourselves fighting on Christmas day, or should I erase it and start over?"

I didn't like the idea of watching my argument with Annie for years to come. "OK, let's both open them together," I suggested.

"Ready, one, two, three!"

Inside the box were three items packed snugly together. One was a tiny golden box of chocolates, the other was a pretty handkerchief with lace trim, and the last was a pocket-sized book titled *How to Order What You Want in Europe*.

I was puzzled. Annie and I looked at each other. "Is this what that phone call was about, Dad?" I asked. "Are we going somewhere soon?"

"That's right. But I was hoping that with these three clues you could guess where we're going."

I thought about it for a few minutes, and then Annie chirped up and took a guess. "France? Are we going to France?"

"Not exactly," Mom said. "But you're pretty close. Farther north and a little bit east."

I got up and ran to the map on the wall in our schoolroom. *North and slightly east of France.* Just above and to the right of France, there was a small country called Belgium (Bell-jum). I ran back into the room.

"Belgium? Are we going to Belgium?"

"Exactly!" Dad said in his best French accent. "It's the place where chocolates, lace, and good food reign supreme."

"Come to breakfast, and we'll tell you all about it," Mom said.

Dad explained that he and Mom had some friends who were missionaries in Belgium.

"Well, the Krogers are really friends of my parents," Dad said. "They provide the Belgian people with good Christian books to read. In fact, they run a printing press right there in Belgium to print the books. They have a bookstore there, too, to sell them."

"It's one of the largest Christian bookstores in Europe," Mom added. "Europe doesn't have lots of

Christian bookstores like we do in the United States."

I thought about how often we go into the Christian bookstore in Chicago to buy a book. It would be terrible not to be able to buy the kinds of books you like to read.

"So this isn't a business trip?" I asked.

"Not exactly. Mr. Kroger asked me to come over and help him solve a mystery."

Annie and I looked sideways at each other with anticipation. We both loved mysteries!

"The people at Good News Fellowship are having trouble with their printing press. They have a very old press that prints all their books and pamphlets." Dad went on to explain that a press is a huge machine with rollers that prints words and pictures onto big sheets of paper. "After it's been printed, the paper is folded and cut into the size of a book by other machines."

He continued. "It seems that someone is stealing or vandalizing parts inside the press. Since it is a holiday week, the Krogers thought I might like to come and take a look. They invited all of us to stay with them."

"This is great!" I said, trying not to sound too happy about the Krogers' troubles.

"This is better than Christmas!" Annie added.

"Well, hopefully. We want it to be a happy new

year for everyone—including the Krogers and Good News Fellowship."

The phone rang. "That's probably Nana and Papa," Mom said, getting up from the table.

Dad answered the phone.

I stopped Mom as she carried the plates back to the counter. "Can I talk to them?" I begged.

"Me too," Annie shouted.

I turned around and glared. "You always want to do the same thing I do. Can't you stop copying me?"

"I'm not copying you. They're my nana and papa, too!"

"Girls, you've got to stop arguing about everything. Now go and pick up your things under the tree. I'm sure your dad and I will be on the phone for a while. Once you've put all your things away upstairs, you may pick up the phone in our room and say hello."

"Me first," Annie giggled as she ran out of the room. "I called it first!"

I looked at Mom and rolled my eyes. I'd just about had it with Annie. Mom says we're just going through a stage, but I wonder. It's not easy getting along. In fact, it's much harder to get along with Annie than with any of my other friends. Mom says that getting along with your sister is a true test of how well you will get along with others. She's probably right. If I can get along with Annie, I can get along with anyone! I picked up my presents and stacked them neatly.

As I walked by the kitchen door, I could hear Mom talking to Nana. "I don't know what it is with those two, Mom. I guess it's just a stage. I don't remember arguing so much with Nancy or Carol. Oh wait. I do remember!" she chuckled. "Maybe it's a good thing we forget!"

Chapter Three

Two days later, we landed at Zaventem Airport, north of the capital city of Brussels. Mr. and Mrs. Kroger were there to greet us with a sign that said *Welcome* in three different languages. Mr. Kroger was a very nice-looking gentleman with wisps of white hair and a friendly smile. He limped a little when he walked and had a habit of pushing his gold-rimmed glasses up the bridge of his nose every time he finished a sentence.

"So, did you girls have a good trip?" he asked, adjusting his glasses.

"It was a fun plane ride, but it seemed kind of long," I replied.

"Well, our clocks are set seven hours ahead of yours at home. Your day will probably seem even longer by tomorrow morning," joked Mrs. Kroger.

She bent down and pulled Annie and me close when she talked. I could tell she liked children.

"Our car is parked out front. I'm afraid we'll really have to crowd in," Mrs. Kroger said. "It's a bit of a drive. I hope you won't be terribly uncomfortable."

At that point, I really didn't care how we got to their house—I was tired and just wanted to get there. It wasn't light yet when we walked out to the car. There really wasn't much to see. *Maybe later on today*, I thought.

"You girls comfortable back there?" Mr. Kroger asked as he turned around and gave Annie and me a big smile.

I tried to sound cheerful even though it was midnight Chicago time. "We're OK. I think we'll just sleep, thank you."

"Could you please wake us up when we get there?" Annie mumbled.

Once the car pulled onto the highway, I realized I couldn't sleep. The lights on the expressway seemed as bright as noon.

"I heard that when astronauts fly over Brussels, they can see the expressway lights from hundreds of miles away," Dad commented.

"Yes," Mr. Kroger replied. "There are so many people paying taxes to Belgium, the government didn't know what to do with all the extra money. They decided to light the whole expressway!"

"Are the lights keeping you awake, girls?" asked Mrs. Kroger.

"Kind of, but that's OK," I answered. I had never met someone so concerned about children. I guess she thought that adults could manage all right on their own.

Belgium was turning out to be pretty interesting. I enjoyed looking at all the road signs. Every one was in two different languages. The Krogers explained that Belgium is made up of two different parts—Flanders, the Flemish side to the north, where they speak Flemish (kind of like Dutch); and Wallonia, the southern part, where they speak French.

"So that's why your welcome sign was in three different languages," Dad nodded.

"Why don't the Belgians just pick one language and stick with it?" I asked. "Are they fighting?"

Mr. Kroger chuckled. "No, they get along most of the time, considering their differences."

I looked at Annie and thought about our differences. *Maybe we're a little like Belgium.* I smiled.

Chapter Four

We finally reached the Krogers' home. *I* hadn't slept for hours, but my *legs* seemed to have taken a nap. When Mr. Kroger opened the car door, I nearly fell out.

Mr. Kroger caught me. "Oops, be careful. Here, let me help you out, Hope."

Ellsworth tumbled out onto the sidewalk right after me. Mr. Kroger reached down and picked him up, too. "Don't forget your . . . I'm sorry, I don't believe we've met. And his name?" After giving his glasses a slight push, Mr. Kroger leaned down and shook Ellsworth's paw.

"His name is Ellsworth," I said, smiling. I liked Mr. and Mrs. Kroger very much. They were the first adults I had met (except for Nana and Papa) who didn't tease me about having a bear.

Curiously, I walked up to the tall, skinny house in front of me.

"We like to say that our town house is an American ranch house that's been turned on its side," Mr. Kroger joked.

When I walked in onto the tile floor, I noticed the house smelled a little musty and felt chilly.

"Just put your bags down here, and we'll take them up to your rooms later," said Mr. Kroger, leading us up the stairs to the main floor of the house.

"Come on into the living room and have something warm to drink," Mrs. Kroger invited.

As dark and cold as the first floor of the house seemed, the second story was warm and friendly. I couldn't get over how clean everything felt and looked, even though it was a little dark without any windows on the sides of the house.

"I thought you might be hungry," Mrs. Kroger said, "so I have a treat here for you—croissants with chocolate inside." She put a plate of crescent-shaped rolls on the coffee table. "My husband is getting coffee for the adults, but I thought you girls might like some hot chocolate."

Hot chocolate sounded great!

"Later on," Mrs. Kroger suggested, "you girls may wish to go outside for a walk or a bike ride. Try to forget that you have skipped a whole night's sleep. That way, you won't have bad jet lag. By tonight, you'll be more than ready to catch up on your sleep."

After our snack, Annie and I were wide awake and thought a bike ride sounded wonderful. The Krogers set out a couple of old bikes for us, and we were on our way to explore the town.

It was the bumpiest bike ride of my life! Annie and I bounced up and down on the cobblestone streets. It was hard to keep our balance, and the baskets on the front of our bicycles rattled so loudly, I was sure everyone was staring at us.

"What's that?" I questioned as we passed a store on the right.

Mrs. Kroger yelled back from the bicycle in front of us. "That's the chemist—you'd call it the drugstore back home."

I could tell what the rest of the stores were just by looking in the windows. There was a bakery and a post office—I could see people walking in with packages to mail. Right next door, there was a grocery store with the letters SARMA on the front.

"We'll stop here, and I'll show you our grocery store," Mrs. Kroger said.

We parked our bikes out front and walked into the store. At the entrance, not far from the cash registers, was a machine where an older woman wearing a scarf stood slicing a long, skinny loaf of bread. Mrs. Kroger explained that when Belgians buy their bread, they cut it and bag it themselves.

We walked around while Mrs. Kroger picked up some cheese, bread, yogurt, and drinking water. After paying for the items, she placed them in her net bag and started out of the store.

"Mrs. Kroger, that doesn't look like enough food for a week."

"Belgians usually buy food for only a day or two, not for a whole week like Americans," Mrs. Kroger explained. "Most people here have very small refrigerators that can't hold much. It's nice to get fresh fruits and vegetables at the market instead of buying everything a week ahead."

I thought it was pretty neat that a person could go grocery shopping and fit it all into a bicycle basket. At home, we pack our trunk full every trip!

On the way back to the Krogers, as Annie was pointing at the orange tiles on the roofs of the houses, her bicycle started to wobble.

Suddenly, a big, black dog raced out in front of her.

"Watch out, Annie!" I yelled. She swerved and quickly hopped off the bike as it landed on the cobblestones with a crash.

"Are you all right, Annie? I'm so sorry about the dog," Mrs. Kroger apologized. "That was Snoops, and it looks like he gave you quite a scare!"

"You mean you know him?" I asked.

"Oh yes, Mr. Kroger and I know almost everyone in the village—even the animals."

As I was picking up Annie's bike, I noticed a beautiful stone church in the middle of the village

square. "Can we take a peek inside that church, Mrs. Kroger?" I asked.

"Of course. Its stained-glass windows are lovely, especially on a sunny day like today. The villagers are quite proud of their church."

As soon as we stepped inside the church and shut the door, the noise from the street disappeared. Even the smallest footstep echoed in the quiet.

Once my eyes adjusted to the dark, I looked up to see the sun streaming through the stained-glass windows above. The sunlight turned every color of the rainbow as it pushed its way through the bright blues, reds, and yellows of the stained glass.

"It's so peaceful," I said in a hush.

Mrs. Kroger put her arm around me and Annie. "It truly is," she said. "But too many people who enter into this peaceful place forget to take that peace with them when they leave."

"What do you mean?" Annie asked.

"Well, as beautiful and peaceful as this church may be, it is just a building. It cannot give us peace that lasts. Only Jesus can do that," she said kindly.

Mrs. Kroger patted me on the shoulder. "We need to be on our way home." She turned to go.

I was glad Jesus lived inside of me and wasn't staying behind in the quiet of the church.

After we were sure Annie's bike was okay, we headed home to prepare an early dinner. By the time dinner was over, both Annie and I were more than ready to head upstairs for bed. The Krogers had told us that they only heated a few rooms in the house—it was really cold upstairs. Annie and I decided to wear our socks to bed and sleep close under the blankets.

I was used to having my own bed, but that night I didn't mind sharing just to keep warm. Sometimes, it isn't so bad to have a little sister.

Chapter Five

The next morning, we woke to the sound of a hard, steady rain beating on the tile roof. I lay in bed with the covers pulled up under my chin and poked Annie in the ribs with my elbow. "Do you hear that, Annie? It sounds like soldiers marching on the roof."

Before she had a chance to answer, the doorbell rang. A loud commotion broke out in the front hallway downstairs. I could hear a boy's voice yelling, "Snoops!" and the barking of what sounded like a very large dog. It sounded as if the boy was trying to get the dog to settle down.

Annie and I looked at each other and yelled, "SNOOPS!"

We grabbed our bathrobes and headed down the stairs to see what was happening. Halfway down the stairs, we stopped. A familiar-looking black dog was slipping and sliding on the tiles in the front hallway.

"Good morning, girls," Mrs. Kroger chirped as she walked by carrying an armful of towels. "Philippe and Snoops are here to make a delivery. You two have met Snoops already. I'm trying to clean him off before he comes up."

Annie and I looked at each other in amazement. Mrs. Kroger seemed so calm as she cleaned up the dirty paw prints all over her floor.

"There you go, Snoops. Now if you can stay out of trouble long enough, you may come up to the kitchen and enjoy a treat." Mrs. Kroger signaled for us to follow.

We climbed the stairs behind Snoops and Mrs. Kroger. "I would like for you girls to meet Philippe. He is nine years old." She said something to Philippe in French. He nodded his head, his wavy, dark brown hair sticking out every which way.

As we sat down at the kitchen table, Philippe reached into the bag he was carrying and took out two yummy-looking pastries. He handed one to each of us and grinned.

"Thank you," I said. I didn't know any French words, so it was going to be hard to talk to him.

"You're welcome," Philippe said back in hard-to-understand English. We smiled at each other.

"Philippe is our next-door neighbor to the left," Mrs. Kroger explained. "His parents own and run the bakery down the street. He delivers baked goods to us on special occasions like today."

She turned to Philippe and asked him a question. He got up and left the table. "He's just going to check the door. But while he's gone, I'll tell you a secret. Philippe is a mischief-maker. He doesn't do too well in school and, unfortunately, he doesn't read very well. I wish he would sit still to read some of the books we give him, but he's too busy. His parents keep him busy delivering things for the bakery."

Philippe walked back in, and Mrs. Kroger handed him a glass of milk. "I'll ask Philippe to take you over to the bakery to deliver these bags to his mother, Madame Tousour."

Mrs. Kroger suggested we run upstairs and throw some clothes on while she talked with Philippe. "Make sure you dress warmly! Here's a hat for each of you." She handed us knit hats that looked like ski masks with a big hole for your face.

Annie made a sour look. "It's all right, Annie, all the kids wear them here," Mrs. Kroger reassured, plopping a red hat down over her frown. Philippe and I laughed.

Before we left, we stopped by Mom and Dad's bedroom. Dad had already left with Mr. Kroger for the Good News Fellowship warehouse. "He'll be there until lunchtime," explained Mom. "Maybe they'll be able to solve the mystery the first day."

"Oh, I hope not," Annie said. "We want to help."

Mom promised us we would visit the warehouse tomorrow. "For now, you two go along with Philippe. But keep him out of trouble—I hear he's a handful."

Philippe was waiting for us at the bottom of the stairs. By his side was Snoops, wagging his tail so hard that the umbrella stand in the corner wobbled.

We grabbed an umbrella and started out the door. The rain had ended, but it looked like it might start again.

At several doors we passed, women were pouring buckets of steaming, soapy water onto the steps. The water then washed down onto the sidewalk as they scrubbed their entryways clean.

"No wonder their houses are so clean," I said to Annie. "They get rid of the dirt before it even has a chance to get tracked in."

Snoops and Philippe started running as the bakery came into view. We hurried behind them until the dog obediently stopped at the corner. He sat by the bakery window and looked in at the beautiful pastries, his tongue hanging out.

Philippe pointed to the woman behind the counter and put his hand to his chest. "Mother," he said in a thick accent. We nodded. He then put his hand up as if to say stop.

We waited outside as Philippe went in. Suddenly, Snoops started to growl. When I looked to see what was wrong, I saw him tugging at a man's pant leg!

The man yelled and jerked his pant leg out of Snoops' mouth, but the dog kept growling.

"Maybe we should get out of here. That man looks mean," Annie said to me in a loud voice.

"It's OK," said the man as he wrapped his black coat around him. "The dog and I know each other. He likes to have a nip at my pant leg now and then. He's just being a bother."

Annie nearly dropped her umbrella on my toe. The man spoke English!

"So, I look mean, do I?" he went on. "Well, perhaps that's why this mutt is always growling at me." Snoops got in one last, low rumble before he turned around and sat next to Annie's feet.

I couldn't tell if the man was kidding or serious. He spoke with a raspy British accent and kept his black hat pulled down over his eyes. It gave me a chill just to look at him.

"Umm . . . I'm sorry . . . but we should probably get into the bakery—to see if we can help with deliveries," I said, backing into the bakery door. "Uh . . . nice to meet you . . . uh . . . sir."

Annie and I turned around, nearly tripping on Snoops. The three of us rushed through the door and into the warm, delicious-smelling store.

What a relief! Then I realized we had just let in a wet dog. I swung open the door and tried to push Snoops out. "Go outside, Snoops. You're not supposed to be in here," I pleaded.

42

Snoops must not have understood English because he didn't budge. Just then, a customer leaned over and offered him a piece of a croissant. I couldn't believe it! I've seen store owners at home give Mom a mean look when she brings *Annie and me* into nice places. Here even dogs were welcomed!

After a few minutes, Philippe came out from behind the counter and motioned for us to follow him outside. We weren't sure we wanted to go out there again. What if that mean-looking Englishman followed us?

I grabbed Annie's sleeve and said in a low voice, "Maybe he's the mystery man who is messing up the Good News Fellowship presses."

Annie pulled a pad out of her pocket and asked me to write down all the details I could remember. I wrote: *Englishman, black raincoat, black hat, teeth marks in pant leg, raspy voice.*

"Put this in your pocket, Annie, and don't let anyone see it." Annie glanced both ways before secretly stuffing the notebook into her pocket.

Maybe we had found our first clue!

Chapter Six

We got back to the Krogers' just in time for a
steaming bowl of leek soup, bread, and
cheese. Mrs. Kroger invited Philippe to stay for
lunch, but he had to leave.

"He wanted to know if you two could play after
lunch. I told him Mr. Kroger was shutting the printing press down for the afternoon to take us all into
the city. Maybe you three can play another afternoon," she suggested. I said I would like that.

Annie and I told everyone at the table about our
adventure that morning. Mr. Kroger was especially
curious about the man in the black hat. "You say he
knew the dog?"

"Not by name," I answered. "But he definitely
talked like he had met him before."

"That's unusual. Tubize is a pretty small village.

Marie and I know nearly everyone here. Have you seen anyone who fits that description, Marie?" he asked with a quick adjustment to his glasses.

"I do remember Isabelle mentioning that a strange Englishman had been by the bookstore a few times lately. What color hair and eyes did you say he has?"

"Well, we didn't get a good look," I said. "He had a large hat on, and it covered his head and face."

"Next time, Detective Brown, try to get more details," Dad teased. He winked at Mom, who had just finished a mystery novel on the flight to Belgium. She loves a mystery as much as I do.

Mr. Kroger went on to explain that we were going to take a bus into the city, then transfer to the metro once we got into town. The metro is like the subway in Chicago, only much cleaner.

Dad had given each of us some Belgian francs to spend. "Now remember to save some to buy a piece of chocolate down by the Grand' Place," he instructed. The Krogers had told us that the Grand' Place is a big market square in the middle of the city. They had some wonderful candy shops there.

As we transferred to the metro from the bus, I

noticed how friendly the people were, especially to Annie and me. I wished I could talk to them—instead I talked to Annie. We hadn't argued much today. I didn't want to make an enemy out of my only English-speaking friend! She must have felt the same way because she stayed awfully close to me.

On the ride there, Dad explained to us that it looked as if someone had been breaking into the Good News Fellowship warehouse and causing the large press to break down. "It's a forty-five-year-old German press, so it's hard to keep it running, anyway. If it weren't for Bill Kroger's understanding of how to fix the press, it probably wouldn't work at all."

"Has anyone figured out how this person is getting into the building?" Mom asked.

"The culprit breaks through a window," Dad answered. "The strange thing is that nothing else has been touched. Nothing's been stolen. Whoever is doing this just makes it impossible for the press to keep printing and for Good News Fellowship to get new books to people."

"Who would want to keep Good News Fellowship from printing books?" I asked. "Books are a good thing. It's not like Good News Fellowship is doing anything wrong."

Mr. Kroger joined the conversation. "But some people think that telling others about Jesus Christ is bad. They'd rather not have those kinds of books or pamphlets around."

I shook my head. All this talk was making me even more determined to find out who had vandalized the press. I took the notebook from Annie and added some more notes: *climbs through window, doesn't steal.*

I thought again about the man in the street with the black coat. Maybe his pant leg was torn for another reason besides Snoops' teeth. Maybe he got it caught on the broken window when he crawled through to damage the press! I wrote a note to myself to check the window for clues when we went to the warehouse tomorrow.

We got off the metro not far from the Grand' Place and followed the Krogers as they led us through the narrow streets. We stopped at what looked like a trailer or an ice-cream stand at a fair, and Dad took out his wallet.

"Here we are, girls. The best fries in the world."

"I love French fries!" Annie exclaimed loudly.

Mom quickly put her hand over her mouth. "They aren't French—they're Belgian. Even the French will admit the Belgians invented fries," Mom said, handing out the fries. They were wrapped in paper cones and topped with a dab of mayonnaise.

"Where's the catsup?" I asked.

"There isn't any. Here's my advice, Hope," Dad said. "When in Belgium, do what the Belgians do. Dig in!"

We arrived at the Grand' Place a few minutes later—a big square where no cars were allowed. It was almost too much to take in at once. In the center of the square stood a large, beautifully decorated Christmas tree full of lights. It was surrounded by a big circle of smaller trees. Like a Maypole, the large tree had ribbons of lights that reached out to the smaller trees. We walked under the canopy of lights. The wet cobblestones shimmered.

Around the square were tall, elegant old buildings which seemed to stand guard over a manger set up to one side. Live animals rested near the display of Mary, Joseph, and baby Jesus. I closed my eyes and listened to the sounds of people's shoes on the cobblestones. Everything was so peaceful without the noisy city traffic. I opened my eyes again. The sun began to set behind the buildings. It was only late afternoon, and already it was getting dark.

"The days are very short in January," Mrs. Kroger remarked.

At that moment, more lights came on, and Annie pointed to the tops of the buildings. "Look, Hope! Oh, isn't it just beautiful?"

All along the square, red-and-green lights shone

from balcony railings. The lights reminded me of my glimmering snowflake ornament at home.

We walked around for a little while longer, and then Dad said that it was time to head back. "Tomorrow we have a long day ahead of us if we're going to help the Krogers solve their mystery."

I turned around to take one last look at the Grand' Place. Squinting at the lights on the tree to make them glisten even more, I looked around the square. If I tried really hard, I could almost imagine what it might have been like to stand there way back in the Middle Ages. I pretended all the people were dressed like monks or merchants.

Mom's voice broke my train of thought. "Hey, dreamer. We need to get going. Did you want to buy a piece of chocolate before we go?"

I felt the Belgian francs in my pocket and nodded.

"If I were you, I'd get a chocolate made with fresh cream and butter. They're especially delicious," Mrs. Kroger advised.

I figured she probably was a good person to listen to, so I asked for one. Annie got a pure chocolate truffle, and Mom and Dad ordered a pound of mixed chocolates. I watched as the lady behind the counter very delicately weighed the chocolates and placed them in a beautiful golden box. Then, she wrapped the box like a Christmas present and tied a gold ribbon around it.

These handmade chocolates sure weren't anything like the ones I found at the bottom of my Christmas stocking!

Chapter Seven

The trip home seemed shorter than the trip into the city. When we got near their home, Mr. Kroger suggested we go ahead and get off the bus near the house. He and Dad were going to walk up to the warehouse to see that nothing had been disturbed since that morning.

"Dad, please be careful," I said before we got off the bus.

"Here. Take my notebook. It might help," Annie said, stuffing the pad into Dad's pocket.

Dad smiled. "Thank you, girls. I am sure I'll be fine. See you at home."

Right before I stepped down off the last step of the bus, I turned back to Dad and reminded him to check the warehouse window for black threads. "The pant leg, Dad. Remember the pant leg!"

When we got back to the house, Annie and I settled into our bedroom and bundled ourselves up for another cold night. I tucked Ellsworth under my arm and held him close. I felt scared and excited all at once. The last thing I wanted to do was fall asleep, so I made hand shadows on the wall next to my bed.

"You see, Ellsworth, the man at the bakery looked like this." I cupped my hands to make my shadow look like a man in a big hat. "In the shadows you will spy the ugly and mysterious guy. . . ." I whispered.

Annie jabbed her elbow into my side. "Stop it, Hope. You're scaring me. What if Dad and Mr. Kroger really *do* find someone in the warehouse?"

At that moment, we heard the front door open downstairs. We grabbed our bathrobes and bolted into the hallway and down the stairs.

"Now just a minute, girls," Dad said. "You're supposed to be in bed." We apologized and begged Dad to give us some details.

"Since you're here, I'll tell you the news. It looks as though someone broke into the building again and cut one of the plastic tubes that picks up the paper and feeds it into the printer. Fortunately, it can be taped up and repaired, but Good News Fellowship will have to buy a replacement. We still don't have a clue who did it."

"Were there any black threads on the window, Dad?" I asked.

"I didn't see any, sweetheart, but we can both look a little more closely tomorrow. For now, you two need to get some sleep."

I watched Mr. Kroger as he locked the front door. I was glad we were safe in their house.

———

After a quick breakfast the next morning, Mrs. Kroger suggested we go down to the bakery and ask Philippe if he'd like to walk down to the warehouse with us. "I thought you girls could encourage Philippe to pick out a book at the store. Maybe you could encourage him to be interested in reading. Run ahead, and we'll pick you three up at the bakery in a few minutes."

I was a little nervous about seeing the man at the corner and was glad when we rounded it and saw no one there. "What a relief!" I said to Annie.

In front of the bakery, we saw Snoops sitting alone, as if he were waiting for us. "Snoops! Snoops!" we both called. The dog just sat there, staring at the baked goods in the window.

"That dog has a one-track mind," Annie joked.

"As far as I'm concerned, he's on the right track," I said, eyeing the chocolate éclairs on the second shelf.

Annie looked at me slyly and giggled. "I see

Snoops isn't the only one with his tongue hanging out!"

We went into the bakery and asked Philippe to come with us to Good News Fellowship. Mrs. Kroger had coached me on how to say the words Good News Fellowship in French. I must have done a pretty good job, because Philippe smiled, grabbed his coat, and headed out the door with us.

"Just in time," Mr. Kroger said as we stepped out onto the sidewalk. "Follow me."

We walked across the street and down the block until we reached a low building with what I guessed were the words *Good New Fellowship* on the side.

"This must be it," I said nervously. I wasn't sure I wanted to go inside. What if the man with the black hat was lurking behind one of the doors?

Once inside, we were greeted by Isabelle, the lady who worked at the bookstore. "Hello," she said, greeting us with a big smile. "Welcome to Good News Fellowship. We're so glad to finally meet you." Her English was very good. I thought how great it would be to speak French that well someday. "Mrs. Kroger told me to make sure you pick out a book before you leave."

She turned to Philippe and offered him a book, too. Philippe seemed very uncomfortable. He stood against the wall and waited while the rest of us looked around.

"Why don't you girls come in and see the press

before we leave?" Mr. Kroger suggested. "We're going to have to rush a bit if we want to take a quick trip to Brugge today to buy that part."

Mr. Kroger led us into the warehouse where the big press stood, as big as an army tank, in the middle of the room. On each side of the huge machine were steps and ladders so the pressman could reach all the handles and levers.

"This is where we make the adjustments to the press," Mr. Kroger explained. The sound of our footsteps on the metal stairs echoed in the big building. He motioned for Philippe to join us, but Philippe shook his head.

"I guess he prefers to stay down below," Dad said.

"If this were a day when the press was running, I'd be shouting at the top of my lungs," Mr. Kroger said. "It can get pretty noisy in here."

"Where's the tube that got cut?" I asked, leaning over the scaffolding.

Mr. Kroger pointed down to where Philippe was standing. "Right down there next to Philippe."

Philippe whirled around on his heels, his face turning snow white. At first, I was sure he had spotted the man with the black hat. I looked around but didn't see anyone.

Mr. Kroger said something to Philippe, and Philippe motioned back that everything was OK.

"I think I caught him a little off guard," Mr. Kroger laughed, adjusting his glasses again.

We all walked down and examined the tube. It was cut clean through.

"Without the vacuum power of this tube, the paper gets off-center," Dad explained. "Eventually, the paper feeder jams."

I still couldn't believe anyone would want to wreck the press. Who would want to keep good books about Jesus from getting out to people?

After a quick look around the rest of the building, Dad and Mr. Kroger decided that nothing else was disturbed. We headed back to the bookstore so Annie, Philippe, and I could pick out a book.

"It will give you something to do on the hour train ride to Brugge," explained Mr. Kroger. He said that he had already talked to Philippe's parents about his going on the trip with us. Snoops had to stay at home.

"Maybe you should have him stand guard at the warehouse," I suggested, turning around to talk to Annie. "He certainly didn't like that nasty man with the—"

Annie shook her head furiously at me, staring straight ahead.

"What's the matter, Annie?"

She just kept shaking her head until I turned around again—only to walk smack into the man with the black hat!

"Oh . . . hello," I said, embarrassed. I couldn't

58

believe it! This was the second time the mysterious man had overheard us talking about him.

The man just grunted and shuffled over to a bookshelf on the back wall of the store.

"That was a close call," I whispered to Annie and Philippe. Annie was holding her sides, trying hard not to laugh.

Chapter Eight

We hurried to choose our books and convinced Philippe to get one, too. He didn't seem too happy about it. Mom and Mrs. Kroger arrived on time, and we headed to the train station.

I loved the train with its big windows and brown bench seats. Philippe and I sat next to each other. Dad and Mom sat in the seat in front of us, and Mr. and Mrs. Kroger sat with Annie across the aisle. As the train pulled out of the station, I picked up my book and settled into my seat for an hour's read. I was glad to have a book with me, since Philippe and I couldn't understand each other.

But not more than five minutes into the book, Philippe punched it from the other side. I lost my grip, and the book fell out of my hands.

"Hey, what's the big idea?" I said in surprise.

Philippe, of course, didn't understand a word. (At least he acted like he didn't.)

Dad saw it happen and gave Philippe a serious, you-had-better-behave-young-man look. Philippe just stared back.

I picked up my book, then handed Philippe his, as if to say, "Why don't you read, too?" He just crossed his arms in front of him and refused to take it.

He sure is stubborn, I thought.

Suddenly, he turned to Mrs. Kroger and blurted out a long stream of French words. I could tell he was pretty frustrated. After he was done, Mrs. Kroger leaned forward and told me that Philippe was not too happy about the train ride—and the books. "He says he hates books because they come between people. He says that even if you spoke the same language, you would probably be more interested in reading your book than in visiting with him."

I sat back and thought about what she'd said. I couldn't imagine not enjoying books. I felt sorry for Philippe—I didn't want to make him feel left out.

I picked up his book and started searching for pictures. I moved to sit next to Philippe, and pointed to the picture of a family having a picnic. "Blue," I said, pointing to the sky.

"*Bleu*," he said in French.

"Basket," I pointed to the picnic basket.

"*Panier*," he said with a smile.

For the rest of the trip, we taught each other words from our own languages. Even though Philippe didn't like to read, he sure had a lot of fun teaching me!

It wasn't too long before we reached Brugge. The town was full of pretty canals. We stopped on a bridge and stood overlooking a row of shops and homes.

"If you come here in the summer, you'll see window boxes overflowing with colorful flowers, and even a cat or two sunning on those rooftops," Mrs. Kroger remarked. It was hard to imagine the warmth of the sun on such a cold and cloudy day. We buttoned up our coats and continued until we reached the little lace shop my mother wanted to visit.

"Nana wouldn't forgive me if I didn't come back with a lace tablecloth for her dining-room table," she said.

A tinkling bell sounded as we walked into the shop. On one side was a long, glass counter filled with lace of every shape and size. On the other side was an older lady dressed in black and white. She wore a white cap on her head and a beautiful lace shawl draped over her shoulders. She was sitting behind a cloth-covered stool. Even though she looked much too old to move very fast, her fingers flew over her work.

"What is she doing?" Annie asked.

"Making lace," Mrs. Kroger explained. She showed us the long, wooden bobbins that were threaded with fine cotton thread and the pattern of pins that held the threads on the cushioned stool.

"See how she twists and ties the bobbins one right after another? She's creating a pattern, the way you do in knitting or crocheting."

"That's right," the woman said in English. "And we've been doing it like this for longer than I've been around."

Annie and I watched while she worked. The dainty pattern she was making reminded me of my snowflake ornament at home. It was a doily to decorate or protect a small table or chest of drawers. I had never seen anything so beautiful and delicate.

"Tell Philippe that it reminds me of a snowflake ornament I have at home on our Christmas tree," I said to Mrs. Kroger. After she told him, he nodded and smiled.

The older lady at the table added, "We don't have as much snow as we do rain here in Belgium, but when it snows, it reminds me of my lace falling to the ground."

I smiled. It was fun to think of snowflakes as little bits of lace.

———

We stopped at a local restaurant for supper before leaving for Tubize. I pulled out my new pocket-sized book I had gotten for Christmas and ordered some tiny potatoes, a lamb chop, and green beans.

On the other side of the table, Philippe sat opening and closing the new Swiss Army pocketknife *he* had gotten for Christmas.

"You better tell Philippe to put that thing away," Mrs. Kroger said to her husband. "He shouldn't be playing with it at the table."

Mr. Kroger whispered to Philippe, and he quickly folded the knife and put it into his pocket.

After we were finished eating, Dad pushed his plate away and declared that he was more than full. "I'm afraid dessert is out of the question!" We all laughed and decided we ought to head home.

"I'm just sorry that tomorrow is our last full day. We still haven't solved the mystery for you," Dad said to Mr. Kroger. Tomorrow was Saturday, and we would be leaving Sunday afternoon after church.

"Well, Reid, it hasn't been a complete waste of time. At least we got up to Brugge so I could get this replacement piece right away," Mr. Kroger said. "Maybe Philippe can put his pocketknife to good use and help me fix it first thing tomorrow morning," he added.

———

It was dark on the way home. Philippe seemed

tired, and Annie had already fallen asleep on Mrs. Kroger's shoulder. I looked out of the train window and stared up at the stars. These were the same stars I had been looking at last week when the carolers came to our door. Maybe they were the same stars my friend Zoe was looking at from her little island of Antigua in the Caribbean. I reached down and felt the charm bracelet I always wore. Zoe had given it to me so I would remember her.

Philippe had fallen asleep, so I was able to think about our unsolved mystery alone. I was almost sure it was the man in the black hat who had caused all the trouble. He was the best suspect we had.

Suddenly, Philippe's book fell from his lap. As I leaned down to pick it up, a thought hit me. *If Philippe really doesn't like books, maybe he cut the tube on the printing press! He even had a knife to do it with.* I didn't want to jump to conclusions, but I decided to tell my idea to Dad in the morning.

Chapter Nine

The next morning, I ran to Mom and Dad's room to share my suspicions about Philippe. I knocked on the door, and Mom answered for me to come in.

"Mom, where's Dad? Is he up yet?" I asked.

"Up yet?! He's already down at the warehouse helping Mr. Kroger fix the press. They picked up Philippe so he could help, too."

"Oh no," I said, landing full force on the bed. "I wanted to go with them."

"They've only been gone about half an hour. If you hurry and eat some breakfast, you can probably go down and watch for a while."

"I don't want to watch them fix the press," I explained. "I want to tell them who vandalized it!"

"Are you sure you know who did it?"

"No, but I think I'm right. Do you mind if I go right down and talk to Dad myself?" I asked. Mom nodded, so I grabbed my coat and ran to the warehouse.

I rushed down the sidewalk, past the bakery, and into the front door of the bookstore. "Excuse me," I said to Isabelle. "But is my dad still here with Mr. Kroger?"

"I believe they're in the warehouse working on the press," she said, pointing to the narrow hallway.

I said thanks and started running down the hall. The closer I got to the warehouse door, the louder the sound of voices became. The loudest sounded like Dad's voice, and he was shouting.

As I opened the door, I saw the backs of Snoops and Philippe. Dad stood facing them. Snoops had tucked his tail between his legs, and Philippe was looking down at the floor.

"Do you realize what trouble you have made for these people?" Dad cried out. "They are trying to do a good thing by printing these books, and you're making it impossible!"

Mr. Kroger was pacing back and forth next to the press. I ran up and stepped right between Dad and Philippe. "Wait a minute, Dad. Philippe can't understand what you're saying, no matter how loud you're saying it."

Dad looked red in the face and more upset than I had seen him look for a long time—almost as angry as I look when I'm fighting with Annie. Philippe started crying. I realized then that Dad had figured out the whole thing—before I could tell him.

Dad backed away, and Mr. Kroger gently put his arm around Philippe and started walking toward the bookstore. It sounded almost like he was comforting him.

"Dad, Philippe didn't mean to be bad. He just gets into trouble sometimes," I said, defending my newfound friend. "I think we might even get him to like books someday."

"You might be right, Hope," Dad said, rubbing his forehead with his hand. "I just can't understand why anyone would do this kind of mischief, I guess. He really got me going."

"Yeah, I noticed," I said. I guess sometimes even dads have a bad day. "By the way, how did you figure out that it was Philippe?"

"I had a hunch last night, so when we came in this morning to fix the press, I was on the lookout for any clues. I remembered that idea you had about the Englishman's pant leg and searching for threads left behind on the window. So I started looking around the scaffolding and ladders to see if I could find even a shred of evidence. I found a shred all right. Take a look at this."

Dad pulled a hunk of dog hair out of his pocket and handed it to me. "If that's not Snoops' hair, I don't know what is," he said.

"So it wasn't such a *hare*brained idea after all?" I giggled.

"It was on the corner of this ladder," Dad said, leaning down to show me. "I guess he took the corner too tightly!"

We both looked at each other and chuckled.

Chapter Ten

At the Krogers' home that evening, we talked about Philippe and the mystery. "What we haven't solved is what to do with Philippe," Dad said.

"Are you going to tell the police?" Annie asked.

"We don't need police to solve this problem," Mrs. Kroger said. "I think Philippe needs a change of heart. I just wish his folks would let him come to church with us. I think he might really enjoy it there."

That night before bed, Annie and I held hands and prayed for Philippe. Afterward I turned to Annie. "Even when there are only two of us praying, the Bible says God is right here with us."

For a long time, Annie and I just lay still next to each other, staring at the ceiling. A few minutes later, Annie broke the silence. "Hope?"

"Yes?" I said.

"I like it when we pray together."

"Me too," I whispered, smiling.

"Good-night, Hope."

"Good-night, Annie."

———

The next morning, we hurried to pack every-thing into the car. We would be going straight to the airport from the morning church service.

Our walk to church took us past the bakery. It was closed, and all the beautiful pastries were gone from the windows. I was disappointed that I hadn't had a chance to say goodbye to Philippe. I hoped he wouldn't be punished too severely for the trouble he had caused at Good News Fellowship.

A few blocks later, we were standing in front of a school building. "Well, here we are at church," Mr. Kroger said in a cheery voice.

"No one told us that you meet in a school," Dad said.

"Yes, it's a far cry from the church in the village with its stained-glass windows, but we have no trou-ble worshiping God here, too."

We walked through an empty hallway. When Mr. Kroger opened the wooden doors into the school auditorium, it was as if he let out the wonderful sound of singing that had been building up inside. Although I couldn't understand anything the people were singing, I knew just the same that they were praising God.

The words were projected onto the wall in front of us. I tried to read them, but finally I gave up and just stood and listened. I enjoyed listening to the sound of the French words. Mr. Kroger stood next to me, writing furiously on a piece of paper. He finally handed it to me. On it were written the English words to the song so I could know what they were singing.

"His name is marvelous, Jesus my King.
He is the Sovereign, Master of the universe.
His name is marvelous, Jesus my King."

The words were a lot like those in a song we sang at home in Chicago.

Just then, Mrs. Kroger nudged me and pointed to the back of the auditorium. There were Philippe and Snoops, standing right next to the back door. I couldn't believe it! We motioned for them to join us. Philippe took off his hat and walked sheepishly up to a chair next to Dad and sat down. Snoops made himself comfortable at Philippe's feet. I reached for

Annie's hand and squeezed it. God had answered our prayer!

We listened as the minister asked the congregation to read aloud the Christmas story. Mrs. Kroger took my Bible and pointed to the second chapter of Luke. As the rest of the congregation read in French, Annie and I followed along in English. "And suddenly there was with the angel a multitude of the heavenly host praising God and saying: 'Glory to God in the highest, And on earth peace, good will toward men.'"

Mr. Kroger handed me a note. "Thank you for praying for Philippe. Maybe now he'll get to know Jesus' peace, too."

After the service was over, Dad and Mr. Kroger left to go get the car. Mom, Annie, and I stayed with Mrs. Kroger to have some refreshments. Philippe was standing next to Mrs. Kroger. He said something to her while taking a small package from his pocket and handing it to me.

Mrs. Kroger translated for us. "Philippe wants to say that he is very sorry for all the trouble he has caused. He also wants you to know that he read the whole book you picked out for him." She added in a whisper, "He had lots of time after he was sent up to his room yesterday.

"He also wanted you to have this, Hope, as a reminder of your friendship."

I took the little package Philippe held out to me

and smiled. "Thank you, Philippe."

"You're welcome," he replied.

Inside the package was another charm for my bracelet. This time it was a beautiful silver snowflake, like the piece of lace the woman in Brugge had been making.

I reached over to Philippe and kissed him once on one cheek, once on the other, and then once again on the first cheek. That was a Belgian thank-you I knew he understood.

Dad and Mr. Kroger came in. It was time to leave for the airport. We said our goodbyes and squeezed back into the Krogers' little car for our ride to the airport.

As we drove away from the school and down the street, I watched Philippe and Snoops standing all alone on the curb. Annie and I waved until we couldn't see them anymore.

I smiled. Even though I couldn't see Philippe, I knew he would *always* be in my heart. This had definitely been the best Christmas ever!

The End